DIANE GOODE'S
Book of
SCARY
Stories & Songs

Dutton Children's Books · New York

TO PETER

Selections collected by Lucia Monfried.
This collection copyright © 1994 by Dutton Children's Books
Illustrations copyright © 1994 by Diane Goode
All rights reserved.
Published in the United States 1994 by
Dutton Children's Books, a division of Penguin Books USA Inc.
375 Hudson Street, New York, New York 10014
Designed by Sara Reynolds
Printed in Hong Kong
First edition
3 5 7 9 10 8 6 4 2

Library of Congress Cataloging-in-Publication Data

Diane Goode's book of scary stories & songs / [illustrated by Diane Goode].
—1st ed.   p. cm.
Summary: A collection of traditional tales, with some poems
and songs, most on a ghostly theme.
ISBN 0-525-45175-7
1. Ghosts—Literary collections.   2. Tales.
[1. Ghosts—Literary collections.   2. Folklore.]
I. Goode, Diane, ill.   II. Title: Book of scary stories and songs.
PZ5.D53   1994   93-32610   CIP   AC

The publisher gratefully acknowledges permission to reprint on:
  page 6, "Spooks A-Hunting," from *A Book of Spooks and Spectres* by Ruth Manning-Sanders.
Text copyright © 1979 by Ruth Manning-Sanders. Reprinted by permission of Harold Ober
Associates, Inc.
  page 21, "No One," copyright © 1975 by Lilian Moore. Reprinted by permission of Marian
Reiner for the author.
  page 22, " 'Tain't So," copyright © 1943, 1946, renewed 1971, 1974 by John Bennett. Reprinted by permission of Russell and Volkening, as agents for the author.
  page 26, "The Man Who Was Afraid of Nothing," from *American Indian Myths and Legends*
by Richard Erdoes and Alfonso Ortiz. Copyright © 1984 by Richard Erdoes and Alfonso
Ortiz. Reprinted by permission of Pantheon Books, a division of Random House, Inc.
  page 32, "The Mermaid," from *Negro Folktales in Michigan*, edited by Richard Dorson.
Text copyright © 1956 by Richard Dorson. Reprinted by permission of Gloria Dorson.
  page 36, "A Ghostly Ballad," from *Heigh-Ho for Halloween!* by Elizabeth Hough Sechrist.
Text copyright © 1948 by Elizabeth Hough Sechrist. Reprinted by permission of Macrae
Smith Co. of Philadelphia.
  page 53, "The House at the Corner," from *Wide Awake and Other Poems* by Myra Cohn
Livingston. Copyright © 1959, renewed 1987 by Myra Cohn Livingston. Reprinted by permission of Marian Reiner for the author.
  page 54, "The Goblins at the Bathhouse," from *A Book of Ghosts and Goblins* by Ruth
Manning-Sanders. Copyright © 1968 by Ruth Manning-Sanders. Reprinted by permission
of Harold Ober Associates, Inc.

Contents

Introduction

PEOPLE HAVE ALWAYS TOLD SCARY STORIES. And others have loved to listen. Ghost stories are among the oldest of supernatural tales. They helped to explain the unknown and, in a world where there has always been so much to fear, to make it seem less frightening. In a story, you have a sense that you have some control over your fright. At the movies, with their combination of horror and delight, you can always pull your coat over your head and scream and hope for the best—or the worst! Or around a campfire, where the dark lies outside the safety of the circle, a scare can be fun.

This book is full of scary fun. When I was a child, the words *ghosts* and *goblins* were magical. I made sure to include lots of them, along with monsters and spooky creatures and settings, in this collection. Some of the stories are also meant to make you laugh at the scariness—by showing that what is supposed to be so scary really isn't.

So if you're ready for some happy shivering, then let's go. Like the boggart in this first story, you wouldn't want to be left behind. You never know who is waiting to get you! LET'S GO!

Once there was a rich farmer who had a fine farm and family. They were very happy except for one thing. There was a boggart in the house.

This boggart was always full of mischief. At night he would pull the covers off the beds. Or he would knock on the door, and when the sleepy farmer went to open it there would be nobody there.

In the daytime he would blow the smoke back down the chimney and cover the farmer's wife full of soot.

Sometimes, however, the boggart would help the family. He washed the dishes when no one was looking and fed and watered the cows and horses. But he usually tied knots in their tails or set them free at night so the poor farmer had to run after them.

The family thought they could enjoy a good prank or two, but this boggart was so annoying that they decided to move to a new house with no boggart.

So they loaded all their belongings on a wagon. Just as they were about to drive off, a tiny voice called from the piled-up furniture, "I'm ready. Let's go!"

Spooks A-Hunting

TIROLEAN

Every year on Saint Martin's Night, the spooks set out for the forest. They ride along the high road, a great company of them, with their three-footed dogs barking and yapping. If you happen to be out and hear them coming, you must fling yourself flat and shut your eyes. Then they will ride over you without hurting you. But woe betide you if you dare to look at them!

And when the hunt passes through a village, the people must go into their houses, shut the doors, draw the curtains, and not peep through the windows until the grand procession has gone by. For the spooks hate prying eyes, and should you venture to look upon them, you will very likely regret it.

Well, in a certain village there was a woman who had more curiosity than sense. She said this tale about the spooks not wishing to be looked at was rubbish; and anyhow how were they to know whether they were being watched or not? She said, moreover, that she *wanted* to see the spooks, and when her chance came along, she was going to take it.

So, on Saint Martin's Night, though she shut her door and drew the curtains, she left the curtains on her bedroom window just a little apart. Then she blew out her candle, sat herself down behind the bedroom curtains, and, through the little gap, peered out into the night.

What did she hear, what did she see?

Before long she heard a *swish, swish, swish* and saw a big birch broom coming along the road all by itself, sweeping the road clean. Then she heard *clump, clump, clump* and saw twelve big shoes stomping along without any feet in them.

And after the twelve big shoes came the Wild Hunt itself: a company of great shadowy riders on great shadowy horses. As the horses galloped by, their feet made no sound at all. A pack of three-legged

dogs, with fiery eyes that lit up the road as they rushed past, followed the horses. Next came a troop of tiny green people, running like the wind and screaming, "Hop! Hop! Hop!"

And last, waddling all by itself, came a bandy-legged goose. And when the woman saw that goose, stretching out its neck and flapping its wings and twiddling its big yellow feet, hurrying to keep up with the rest of the procession—well, she burst out laughing.

And what did the goose do then?

It stepped aside and gave a peck at the woman's garden fence. Then it *flap-flapped* down the road after the riders.

"Oh, oh, oh!" the woman shrieked. For, although the goose had only pecked at the garden fence, the woman felt the goose's beak pecking at her left leg, as if a sharp pair of scissors had been driven into her. As the days went by, the pain got worse, until she grew lame. Lame she was, and lame she remained for a whole year.

Then came Saint Martin's Night again. The woman didn't peep out from between her bedroom curtains this year. The house was dark, and she sat before her kitchen fire with her sore leg up on a stool, for the pain in her leg had never been worse. So she didn't see the birch broom sweeping the road, nor the twelve big shoes

stomping along, nor the shadowy riders on their shadowy horses, nor the fiery-eyed dogs, nor the tiny green people, nor the bandy-legged goose flapping its wings at the tail of the procession.

But now the goose spoke in such a loud, clear voice that even though the doors and windows were shut, the woman could hear every word that the goose was saying.

"Last year I stuck a hook in this fence. Now I'll take it out."

Then the goose stepped over to the woman's garden fence, gave a peck, and pulled out something that looked like a little silver fish-hook.

Hey, presto! Suddenly the pain vanished from the woman's leg, and she jumped up, opened the window, and leaned out.

"Oh, thank you, thank you, dear goose!" she cried.

And the goose answered:

> *"Eyes that see more than they should*
> *Will never bring their owner good.*
> *But she who's learned this lesson right*
> *Need not fear Saint Martin's Night."*

And then it waddled away along the road, with its neck stretched out and its wings flapping, in a hurry to catch up with the grand procession.

My Big Toe

TRADITIONAL

There was once an old man and an old woman. They were very poor, but they always had food, because they grew potatoes in the little patch at the edge of their house. One day the old woman was digging in the potato patch, and she dug up something that looked like a giant potato. She decided she would surprise her husband and make his favorite food, potato soup, for supper.

That night after supper the old woman and the old man went to bed. They were just about asleep when they heard a strange noise. It said, "I want my big toe. I want my big toe."

The old woman asked the old man to get up and see what it was, but the old man was scared, and he told the old woman to get up.

So the old woman got up. She searched through the house but didn't see anything, so she went back to bed.

A little while later they heard the strange noise again. This time the old man got up. He looked around and thought he saw something behind the kitchen table. He got so scared that he ran and jumped back in bed.

Then the old woman went into the kitchen and said, "I'll give you what's left of the soup if you'll go away." The old woman placed the soup on the table, and then she ran back to bed.

But from then on she never made potato soup again.

The Pumpkin Giant

AMERICAN

A very long time ago there were no pumpkins. No one had baked a pumpkin pie or made a jack-o'-lantern. That was the time when the Pumpkin Giant lived.

The Pumpkin Giant was taller than any other giant. He had a great round head, all smooth and shiny. His eyes glowed like coals in his head. His mouth stretched halfway around his head. The giant lived in a castle, and all around the castle was a moat filled with bones. He was fond of eating little boys and girls, most particularly fat little boys and girls.

The fear and terror of the Pumpkin Giant had spread over the whole country, even to the king on his throne. And the poor king had reason to shake; his only daughter, the princess Ariadne Diana, was the fattest little girl the world had ever seen. So fat was she that she never walked a step. The only way she could get around was by stretching herself out on the earth and rolling. Whenever the princess went rolling, fifty soldiers went along with her, but even so the king was worried.

An old man with little to his name but the potato field he worked and the roof over his head lived not far from the Pumpkin Giant's castle. And this old man had a son who was fatter than the princess Ariadne Diana.

One morning the farmer and his fat son were out in the potato field, digging up a new crop of potatoes. Suddenly they felt the earth rumble under their feet. They looked up, and there, striding toward them with his mouth wide open and his eyes glowing like coals, was the Pumpkin Giant.

"Get behind me, son. Hide yourself," said the farmer.

The boy rolled behind his father and tried to hide himself, but it did little good, for his fat cheeks stuck out on either side of his father's waistcoat.

The Pumpkin Giant came closer and closer, and his big mouth opened wider and wider, until they could almost hear it crack at the corners.

When the Pumpkin Giant was right before them, the farmer reached down in the basket of potatoes, picked out the largest one he could find, and threw it straight down the Pumpkin Giant's throat. The Pumpkin Giant choked and gasped, and then fell over. His head smashed as it hit the ground, and pieces flew all over the field.

News of the death of the Pumpkin Giant was brought to the king, and he was greatly relieved. The princess Ariadne Diana was allowed to go rolling without the fifty soldiers getting in the way.

The next spring, instead of potatoes in his field, the farmer had queer green running vines in every nook and corner. And in the fall there grew on the vines yellow Giant's heads—hundreds of them! The people were thrown into consternation.

"If the Giant's heads have grown on the vines," they said, "then Giant's bodies will follow. And what will we do with an army of Pumpkin Giants?"

But after a while all the excitement died down, for bodies did not grow on the vines and the heads showed no signs of developing mouths. Soon everybody forgot about the queer crop in the farmer's garden.

Everybody except the farmer's son. He watched those Giant's heads get bigger and bigger and yellower and yellower, until one day he could stand it no longer. He rolled into the kitchen, got the carving knife, rolled out into the potato field, cut a piece out of a Giant's

head, and stuffed it in his mouth. He was a little afraid it might make him sick. But the Giant's head tasted good, and he ate and ate.

"See now, son, what you have done!" his parents said. "Surely you will die!" And they sat down and wept.

But he didn't die. "I've never felt better in my life—except I'm still hungry," he said. "I'm going out into the potato field for a Giant's head, and we all shall eat it."

"No!" said his parents.

But the boy had already rolled out into the potato field, and when he came back, he had a great round yellow Giant's head in his arms. They all tasted it, and they said it was good.

"But," said the farmer's wife, "it would be better if it were cooked." She mixed the Giant's head with eggs and milk, sugar and spices, poured the mixture into a piecrust, and put it in the oven. When she took it out an hour later, she had a spicy, sweet golden brown pumpkin pie.

So every day after that she baked pumpkin pies. It happened that the king was riding by the cottage and sniffed the sweet, spicy smell of baking pumpkin pies.

"What smells so good?" said the king. A piece of pie was brought to him. When he tasted it, he declared he had never eaten anything half so good. He ordered the farmer's wife to tell him how the pies were made, and she told the king the whole story of the Giant's death.

When the king returned to the palace that day, the farmer and his family went with him. All the roses in the royal gardens were uprooted and pumpkins planted in their place.

The farmer became the head gardener; his wife baked the pies; and their son—why, he did nothing but eat them, with the princess Ariadne Diana.

In time the farmer's son and the princess were married. It took fifty archbishops to perform that marriage, and the newspapers said there had never been such a well-matched couple as the two of them when they rolled down the aisle after the ceremony.

Someone

Someone came knocking
  At my wee, small door;
Someone came knocking,
  I'm sure-sure-sure;
I listened, I opened,
  I looked to left and right,
But nought there was a-stirring
  In the still dark night;
Only the busy beetle
  Tap-tapping in the wall,
Only from the forest
  The screech owl's call,
Only the cricket whistling
  While the dewdrops fall,
So I know not who came knocking,
  At all, at all, at all.

Walter de la Mare

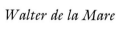

No One

In this room
there's not a
breeze.

No one sneezed
the littlest
sneeze.

No one wheezed
the faintest
wheeze.

The door's shut
tight
with a big brass
handle.

Who?
WHO
BLEW OUT THE CANDLE?

Lilian Moore

'Tain't So

Old Mr. Dinkins was taken ill very suddenly, so they sent for the doctor in a big hurry. When he came, old man Dinkins said, "There's nothing the matter with me!"

"You are dying," said the doctor.

" 'Tain't so!" said old man Dinkins. But the next day he was dead.

So they put the old man in his coffin; they carried him to church and had his funeral; then they carried him to the graveyard and buried him. They put up a gravestone, but there was no time to carve anything on it, not even his name.

The next morning a neighbor passing the graveyard on his way to work saw old man Dinkins sitting on the graveyard fence.

"Hello there! I thought you were dead," said the neighbor.

" 'Tain't so!" said old man Dinkins.

The neighbor went and told old Mrs. Dinkins that her husband was sitting on the graveyard fence, saying he was not dead.

"Pay no attention," said the widow. "He's foolish."

Later on another neighbor passing by the graveyard heard someone say, "Hello, Tom!"

"Hello," said Tom, and stopped for a chat. "It's you, is it?"

"Sure," said old man Dinkins.

"I heard you were dead."

" 'Tain't so!"

"I heard about the burial."

"Well, you can see I'm not buried."

"That's so," said the neighbor, and went on, somewhat puzzled.

The next day someone from town was passing by the graveyard on horseback. He heard someone say "Hello" and stopped to see who it was. He saw a very old gentleman sitting on the fence. The old gentleman said, "What's the news from town?"

"Not much news, except old man Dinkins is dead."

" 'Tain't so!"

"That's what they said."

"Well, 'tain't so."

"How do you know?" said the man.

"I'm Dinkins."

"Oh!" said the man, and rode away pretty fast. He stopped at the nearest store and said, "There's a funny old fellow sitting on the graveyard fence who says he is old man Dinkins."

"Can't possibly be," said the storekeeper.

"Why not?"

"Because old man Dinkins is dead."

This kept going on week after week, month after month. The whole town knew that old man Dinkins was dead; but old man Dinkins sat on the graveyard fence saying, " 'Tain't so."

After much talk and consultation the townspeople decided to hold another burial. But first they had these words carved on the gravestone:

HERE LIES
THE BODY OF
THEODORE DINKINS
AGED 91
RESPECTED CITIZEN OF
WADMALOW ISLAND
WHO DIED
JANUARY 17, 1853

Then they said the burial service over the old man's grave for a second time.

The next day when old man Dinkins crawled out of his grave, he read what the stone said. He read it over two or three times.

"Well—maybe so," he said. He hasn't yelled at anybody from the graveyard fence since then.

The Man Who Was
Afraid of Nothing

NATIVE AMERICAN

There were four ghosts sitting together, talking, smoking ghost smoke, and having a good ghost time. One of them said: "I've heard of a young man nothing can scare. He's not afraid of us, so they say."

The second ghost said: "I bet we could scare him."

The third ghost said: "We must try to make him afraid."

The fourth ghost said: "Let's make a wager. Whoever can scare him the most, wins." And they agreed.

Soon this young man who was never afraid came walking along. The moon was shining. Suddenly in his path the first ghost materialized, taking the form of a skeleton. "Hou, friend," said the ghost, clicking his teeth together, making a sound like a water drum.

"Hou, cousin ghost," said the young man, "you're in my way. Get off the road and let me pass."

"Not until we have played the hoop-and-stick game. If you lose, I'll make you into a skeleton like me."

The young man laughed. He bent the skeleton into a big hoop, tying it with some grass. He took one of the skeleton's leg bones for his game stick and rolled the skeleton along.

"Ouch!" said the skeleton. "You're hurting me."

"Well, you asked for it. Who proposed this game, you or me? You're a silly fellow." The young man kicked the skeleton aside and walked on.

Farther on he met the second ghost, also in the form of a skeleton, who jumped at him and grabbed him with bony hands. "Let's dance, friend," the skeleton said.

"A very good idea, cousin ghost," said the young man. "What shall we use for a drum and drumstick? I know!" He took the ghost's thighbone and skull and danced and sang, beating on the skull with the bone.

"Stop, stop!" cried the skull. "This is no way to dance. You're hurting me; you're giving me a headache."

"You're lying, ghost," said the young man. "Ghosts can't feel pain. There we were, having a good time, and you spoiled my fun with your whining." The young man scattered the bones all over.

"Now see what you've done," complained the ghost. "It will take me hours to get all my bones together. You're a bad man."

"Stop your moaning," said the young man. Then he went on.

Soon he came upon the third ghost, another skeleton. "This is getting monotonous," said the young man. "Are you the same ghost as before? Did I meet you farther back?"

"No," said the ghost. "Those were my cousins. They're soft. I'm tough. Let's wrestle. If I win, I'll make you into a skeleton like me."

"My friend," said the young man, "I don't feel like wrestling with you. I feel like sledding, and I'll use your rib cage for it."

The young man took the ghost's rib cage and used it as a sled. "This is fun!" he said, whizzing down the hill.

"Stop, stop," cried the ghost's skull, "you're breaking my ribs!"

The young man said: "Friend, you look funny without a rib cage. You've grown so short. Here!" And he threw the ribs into a stream.

"Look what you've done! What can I do without my ribs? I need them."

"Jump in the water and dive for them," said the young man. "You look as if you need a bath." He walked on.

Then he came upon the chief ghost, a skeleton riding a skeleton horse. "I've come to kill you," said the skeleton.

The young man made faces at the ghost. He rolled his eyes; he showed his teeth and gnashed them; he made weird noises. "I'm a ghost myself, a much more terrible ghost than you are," he said.

The skeleton got scared and tried to turn his ghost horse, but the young man seized it by the bridle. "A horse is just what I want," he said. "Get off!" He yanked the skeleton from its mount and got on the skeleton horse and rode it into camp. Day was just breaking, and some villagers saw him and screamed loudly, waking everyone else. The people looked out of their tepees and became frightened when they saw him on the ghost horse. As soon as the sun appeared, however, the horse vanished. The young man laughed.

The story of his ride on the skeleton horse was told all through the camp. The young man bragged about putting the four skeleton ghosts to flight. People shook their heads, saying, "This young man is really brave. Nothing frightens him. He is the bravest man who ever lived."

Just then a tiny spider crawled up the young man's sleeve. When someone called his attention to it, he cried, "Eeeeech! Get this bug off me! Please, someone take it off, I can't stand spiders! Eeeeech!" He shivered, he writhed, he carried on, until a little girl laughed and took the spider off him.

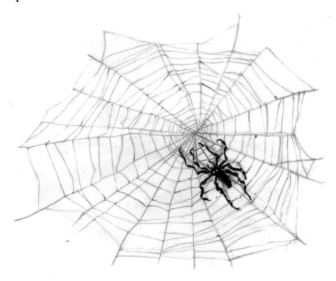

The Mermaid

Before they had any steam, ships were going by sails across the Atlantic. The Atlantic was fifteen miles deep, and there were mermaids in those days. And if you called anybody's name on the ship, the mermaids would ask for it. They would say, "Give it to me." And if you didn't give it to them, they would capsize the ship.

So the captain had to change the men's names to different objects —hatchet, ax, hammer, furniture. Whenever he wanted a man to do something, he had to call him, "Hammer, go on deck and look out."

The mermaid would holler, "Give me Hammer." So they threw the hammer overboard to her, and the vessel would proceed on.

The captain might say, "Ax, you go on down in the kindling room and start a fire in the boiler; it's going dead."

Then the mermaid says, "Give me Ax." So they have to throw her an ax.

Next day he says, "Suite of Furniture, go down in the stateroom and make up those beds."

And the mermaid yells, "Give me Suite of Furniture." So they had to throw a whole suite of furniture overboard.

One day the captain made a mistake and forgot and said, "Sam, go in the kitchen and cook supper."

The mermaid right away calls, "Give me Sam." They didn't have anything on the ship that was named Sam, so they had to throw Sam overboard.

Soon as Sam hit the water the mermaid grabbed him. Her hair was so long she could wrap him up—he didn't even get wet. And she's swimming so fast he could catch breath under the water. When she get him home, she unwraps Sam out of her hair, says: "Oooh, you sure do look nice. Do you like fish?"

Even though Sam wouldn't cook a fish, they were married. But after a while Sam begin to step out with other mermaids. One of

Sam's new girlfriends was jealous of him and his wife, and the mermaids had a fight over Sam. The wife whipped the girlfriend and told her, "You can't see Sam never again."

But the girlfriend says, "I'll get even with you."

So one day Sam's girlfriend asked him, didn't he want to go back to his native home. He says yes. So she grabs him, wraps him in her hair, and swims the same fastness as Sam's wife did when she was carrying him, so he could catch breath. When she come to land she put Sam onto the ground on the bank. "Now if he can't do me no good, he sure won't do her none."

That was Sam's experience in the mermaid's house in the bottom of the sea.

A Ghostly Ballad

Elizabeth Hough Sechrist

Deep in a wood An old hut stood, Where lived a her - mit

all a-lone. Now, time had brought This old man nought, He

lived on bits of bread and bone. O - o - oh!

One night he walked
Where ghosts oft stalked
Upon the crest of wooded hill.
The chill winds moaned
And sighed and groaned,
The night was dark, and darkly still!
O-o-oh!

He reached the top
And there did stop
To rest upon an old dead tree.
With weird wild cries,
Before his eyes
Appeared a ghost, plain as could be.
O-o-oh!

From where he sat
Cried: "What is that?
Ye ghastly ghost, get gone, beldame!"
The ghost began
To clutch his hand,
And whispered, *(End with a shriek!)*

The Worms Crawl In

The worms crawl in, The worms crawl out. The worms play

pi - noch - le On your snout. They turn your guts To

sau - er - kraut. They slime your skin as They crawl a - bout.

Another way to start this song is by singing the verse below as the first verse.

Don't you ever laugh   They wrap you up
As the hearse goes by,   In a big white sheet,
For you may be   And drop you down
The next to die.   Ten feet deep.

Dauntless Little John

ITALIAN

There was once a lad called Dauntless Little John, because he was afraid of nothing. One day on his travels, he came to an inn and asked for lodgings. "We have no room here," said the innkeeper, "but if you're not afraid, I will direct you to a certain palace where you can stay."

"Why should I be afraid?" asked Little John.

"Nobody who has gone in has come out alive," answered the innkeeper. But Little John was not afraid. He picked up a lamp, a bottle, and a sausage, then marched straight to the palace.

Night came, and he was having his supper at the table in front of the great fireplace when he heard a voice in the chimney. "Shall I throw it down?"

"Go ahead!" replied Little John.

Down the chimney into the fireplace fell a man's leg.

Then the voice spoke again. "Shall I throw it down?"

"Go ahead!" Another leg dropped into the fireplace.

"Shall I throw it down?"

"By all means!" And there was an arm, and then another arm.

"Shall I throw it down?"

"Yes!"

Then came the trunk of a body, and the arms and legs stuck onto it, and there stood a man without a head.

"Shall I throw it down?"

"Throw it down!"

Down came the head and sprang into place on top of the trunk. It was truly a giant! Was Little John afraid? No! He raised his glass and said, "Good evening."

The giant said, "Take the lamp and come with me."

Little John picked up the lamp but didn't budge. "No, after you," he insisted.

So the giant went first, with Little John behind him, lighting the way. They went through room after room until they came to a staircase. Beneath it was a small door.

"Open it!" ordered the giant.

"You open it!" replied Little John.

So the giant shoved it open with his shoulder. Winding down into the darkness was a spiral staircase.

"Go on down," directed the giant.

"After you," answered Little John.

They went down the steps into a cellar, and the giant pointed to a stone slab on the ground. "Raise that!"

"You raise it!" replied Little John.

The giant lifted it.

Beneath the slab were three pots of gold, which the giant carried up.

When they were back in the hall with the great fireplace, the giant said, "Little John, the spell has been broken!" At that, one of his legs came off and kicked its way up the chimney. "One of these pots of gold is for you." An arm came loose and rose up the chimney. "The second pot of gold is for the friars who will come to carry away your body, believing you have perished here." The other arm came off and followed the first. "The third pot of gold is for the first poor man who comes by." Then the other leg floated up. "Keep the palace for yourself." The trunk separated from the head and vanished. "No one will ever haunt this palace again." At that, the head disappeared up the chimney.

As soon as it was light, the friars appeared to carry off Little John's body. But there he stood, at the window, eating his sausage!

Dauntless Little John was a wealthy young man indeed with all those gold pieces, and he lived happily in his palace.

The Conjure Wives

AFRICAN-AMERICAN

nce on a time, when a Halloween night came on the dark o' the moon, a lot o' old conjure wives was a-sittin' by the fire an' a-cookin' a big supper for theirselves.

The wind was a-howlin' round like it does on Halloween nights, an' the old conjure wives, they hitched theirselves up to the fire an' talked about the spells they was a-goin' to weave long come midnight.

By an' by there come a knockin' at the door.

"Who's there?" called an old conjure wife. "Who? Who?"

"One who is hungry and cold," said a voice.

Then the old conjure wives, they all burst out laughin', an' they called out:

> "We's a-cookin' for ourselves.
> Who'll cook for you?
> Who? Who?"

The voice didn't say nothin', but the knockin' just kept on.

"Who's that a-knockin'? Who? Who?" called out another conjure wife.

Then there come a whistlin', wailin' sound:

> "Let me in, do-o-o-o!
> I'se cold thro-o-o-o an' thro-o-o-o,
> An' I'se hungry too-o-oo!"

Then the old conjure wives, they all burst out laughin', an' they commenced to sing out:

> "Git along, do!
> We's a-cookin' for ourselves.
> Who'll cook for you?
> Who? Who?"

The voice didn't say nothin', but the knockin' just kept on.

Then the old conjure wives, they went to work a-cookin' the supper for theirselves, an' the voice didn't say nothin', but the knockin' just kept on.

An' then the old conjure wives, they hitched up to the fire an' they ate an' they ate, an' the voice didn't say nothin', but the knockin' just kept on. An' the old conjure wives, they called out again:

"Go 'way, do!
We's a-cookin' for ourselves.
Who'll cook for you?
Who? Who?"

An' the voice didn't say nothin', but the knockin' just kept on.

Then the old conjure wives began to get scared-like, an' one of 'em says, "Let's give it somethin' an' get it away before it spoils our spells."

An' the voice didn't say nothin', but the knockin' just kept on.

Then the old conjure wives, they took the littlest piece of dough, as big as a pea, an' they put it in the fry pan.

An' the voice didn't say nothin', but the knockin' just kept on.

An' when they put the dough in the fry pan, it begun to swell, an' it swelled over the fry pan an' it swelled over the top o' the stove an' it swelled out on the floor.

An' the voice didn't say nothin', but the knockin' just kept on.

Then the old conjure wives got scared an' they ran for the door, but the door was shut tight.

An' the voice didn't say nothin', but the knockin' just kept on.

An' then the dough, it swelled an' it swelled all over the floor, an' it swelled up into the chairs. An' the old conjure wives, they climbed up on the backs of the chairs, an' they were scareder and scareder. An' they called out, "Who's that a-knockin' at the door? Who? Who?"

An' the dough kept a-swellin' an' a-swellin', an' the old conjure wives begun to scrooge up smaller an' smaller, an' their eyes got bigger an' bigger with scaredness, an' they kept a-callin', "Who's that a-knockin'? Who? Who?"

An' then the knockin' stopped, and the voice called out:

"Fly out the window, do!
There's no more house for you!"

An' the old conjure wives, they spread their wings an' they flew out the windows an' off into the woods, all a-callin', "Who'll cook for you? Who? Who?"

An' now if you go into the woods in the dark o' the moon, you'll see the old conjure wife owls an' hear 'em callin', "Who'll cook for you? Who-o! Who-o!"

Only on a Halloween night you don't want to go round the old owls, because then they turns to old conjure wives a-weavin' their spells.

Mr. Miacca

ENGLISH

Tommy Grimes was sometimes a good boy and sometimes a bad boy, and when he was a bad boy, he was a very bad boy. His mother used to say to him:

"Tommy, Tommy, be a good boy, and don't go out of our street, or else Mr. Miacca will get you."

But still, on the days when he was a bad boy, he would go out of the street. One day, sure enough, he had scarcely got round the corner when Mr. Miacca caught him and popped him into a bag, upside down, and took him off to his house.

When Mr. Miacca got Tommy inside the house, he pulled him out of the bag, set him down, and felt his arms and legs.

"You're rather tough," says he, "but you're all I've got for supper,

and you'll not taste bad boiled. But body o' me, I've forgotten the herbs, and it's bitter you'll taste without herbs. Sally! Here, I say, Sally!" And he called Mrs. Miacca.

"What d'ye want, my dear?" says she.

"Oh, here's a little boy for supper," says Mr. Miacca, "but I've forgotten the herbs. Mind him, will ye, while I go for them."

"All right, my love," says Mrs. Miacca. And off he goes.

Then Tommy Grimes says to Mrs. Miacca: "Does Mr. Miacca always have little boys for supper?"

"Mostly, my dear," says Mrs. Miacca, "if little boys are bad enough and come his way."

"And don't you have anything else but boy meat? No pudding?" asks Tommy.

"Ah, I loves pudding," says Mrs. Miacca, "but it's not often the likes of us gets pudding."

"Why, my mother is making a pudding this very day," says Tommy Grimes, "and I'm sure she'll give you some if I ask her. Shall I run and get some?"

"Now, that's a thoughtful boy," says Mrs. Miacca, "only don't be long and be sure to be back in time for supper."

So off Tommy pelted, and right glad he was to get off! After that he was as good as good could be. He remembered his mother's words, and he remembered being popped into Mr. Miacca's bag, and he never went round the corner out of the street.

But somehow he couldn't always remember to be good. And one day he went round the corner again, and, as luck would have it, Mr. Miacca was there and grabbed him up, popped him in his bag, and took him home.

When Mr. Miacca opened the bag and saw who it was, he says:

"Ah, you're the youngster that served me and my missus such a shabby trick, leaving us without any supper! Well, you shan't do it again. I'll watch over you myself. Here, get under the sofa, and I'll sit on it and watch the pot boil for you."

So poor Tommy Grimes had to creep under the sofa, and Mr. Miacca sat on it and waited for the pot to boil. And they waited and they waited, but still the pot didn't boil, till at last Mr. Miacca got tired of waiting, and he says:

"Here, you under there, I'm not going to wait any longer. Put out your leg, and I'll stop you giving me the slip."

So Tommy put out a leg, and Mr. Miacca got out a chopper and chopped it off and popped it in the pot. Suddenly he calls out:

"Sally, my dear! Sally!" and nobody answered. So he went into the next room to look for Mrs. Miacca, and while he was gone, Tommy crept out from under the sofa and ran out the door. For you see, it wasn't his own leg but the leg of the sofa that he had put out.

So Tommy Grimes ran home, and he never went round the corner again until he was old enough to go alone.

The Gobble-uns'll Git You Ef You Don't Watch Out!

Little Orphant Annie says, when the blaze is blue,
An' the lamp-wick sputters, an' the wind goes *woo-oo!*
An' you hear the crickets quit, an' the moon is gray,
An' the lightnin'-bugs in dew is all squenched away,—
You better mind yer parunts, an' yer teachurs fond an' dear,
An' churish them 'at loves you, an' dry the orphant's tear,
An' he'p the pore an' needy ones 'at clusters all about,
Er the Gobble-uns'll git you
    Ef you
      Don't
        Watch
          Out!

James Whitcomb Riley

The Ghost of John

Have you seen the ghost of John?
Long white bones
and the flesh all g-o-n-e?
Oooooooooh!
Wouldn't it be chilly
with no skin o-n?

The House at the Corner

The house at the corner
is cold gray stone,
where the trees and windows
crack and groan,
so I run past
      fast
         when I'm all alone.

Myra Cohn Livingston

The Goblins
at the Bathhouse

ESTONIAN

Long ago, in a little town, there was a young girl who worked in the bathhouse. Everyone loved her because she was so kind and helpful.

Late one night, as she was tidying up, she heard a rattling of wheels and a clatter of hooves in the street.

She ran to open the door and saw a magnificent golden coach drawn by four black stallions.

Surely this must be the wedding coach of some rich lord, thought the girl.

But instead, out stepped a hideous little goblin man with glaring eyes and bandy legs. And after him came a younger goblin even uglier, followed by an old, old goblin woman.

The girl quickly ran back into the bathhouse and slammed the door.

"Go away, go away, go away!" she whispered under her breath.

But the goblins didn't go away. The hideous little goblin man called out, "Come out here to me, my little daughter. Your bridegroom awaits you! I have chosen you as wife for my son."

The girl was very frightened, but she kept her wits about her, and she called back, "I'm not ready to be married. I have no shoes or clothes."

The goblin man called, "Tell me what clothes you need, my little daughter, and you shall have everything your heart desires."

As the girl stood thinking of what to say next, a little mouse crept up to her and whispered, "Listen, don't be in a hurry. Tell the goblin what clothes you need, but tell him slowly, a garment at a time. When dawn comes, the goblins will flee."

So the girl called out, "First of all I need a silk chemise."

The young goblin leaped and vanished. He was here, he was there, he was back again, holding in his claws a silk chemise.

The old goblin woman threw it in through the bathhouse window. "Here is your silk chemise, little daughter. Put it on and let us go, for the wedding bells are ringing under the earth."

"Take your time. The dawn is still far off," whispered the little mouse. And the girl slowly put on the silk chemise.

"Is the silk chemise to your liking, little daughter?" called the old goblin woman.

"Yes, it is to my liking," said the girl. "But I am not ready. I have no golden gown."

The young goblin leaped and vanished; then he was back again, carrying in his claws a golden gown.

The old goblin woman tossed the golden gown in through the window of the bathhouse. And the little mouse whispered to the girl, "Slow down! The dawn is not here yet."

The girl slowly put on the golden gown. And the old goblin woman called from outside the door, "Is the golden gown to your liking, little daughter?"

"Yes, it is to my liking," said the girl.

"Then come out, little daughter," called the old goblin woman, "for under the earth the wedding feast is spread."

"But I am not ready," said the girl. "I lack a pair of silver slippers."

The young goblin leaped and vanished. He was here, he was there, he was back again, carrying the silver slippers.

The old goblin woman tossed the silver slippers in through the window of the bathhouse.

"Linger!" whispered the little mouse to the girl. "The dawn comes slowly." So she slowly put on the silver slippers.

"Are the slippers to your liking, little daughter?" called the old goblin woman.

"Yes, they are to my liking," said the girl.

"Then come, little daughter. We cannot wait longer."

"You will have to go out now," whispered the little mouse to the girl. "But take your time. For the dawn is at hand."

So the girl opened the bathhouse door and stepped out. There she stood on the threshold, looking like a king's daughter. The goblin man opened the coach door and stretched out a bony hand to help her inside.

But the girl drew back. "Oh, no, the coach is not to my liking! I am not used to traveling on feather cushions. I must have the coach strewn with hay."

The old goblin struck his hands together. "What can we do? Down under the earth there is no hay!"

The girl looked up. Was there a glimmer of dawn in the sky?

"I ride on hay or not at all," she said.

The goblins began to scream and chatter. The old goblin woman took out her eyes and flung them up into the air. They whirled around in a circle and came back into her head.

"I have seen hay," the old goblin woman shrieked. "In a field outside the big city. Leap, leap, and bring hay."

The young goblin leaped and vanished but did not return. The goblins screamed and danced with impatience.

Finally a huge bundle of hay came rolling along the street and stopped beside the bathhouse. And from under the bundle crawled the young goblin, panting. The other goblins grabbed up the hay in armfuls and began stuffing it into the coach.

"Hurry, hurry, hurry!" they screamed, tumbling over each other. "Dawn is coming!"

They had the hay in the coach at last. The old goblin man seized the girl by the arm. "Get in!" he yelled.

"You first," said the girl. The goblins crowded into the coach. The old goblin man stretched out his hand to help the girl in. The girl glanced up at the sky. Yes, in the east the dawn was breaking.

Cock-a-doodle-do! All the cocks in the little town began to crow. At that sound, coach, horses, old goblin man, old goblin woman, and young goblin gave one last despairing yell and vanished.

The girl stood alone at the bathhouse door. Her golden gown and her silver shoes glistened in the dawn light. The little mouse crept out of the bathhouse, stood up on its hind legs, and squeaked, "Well done, my lovely one."

So the girl took the little mouse up in her hand and went home.

The Green Ribbon

TRADITIONAL

Once there was a little girl named Jenny. She was like all the other girls, except for one thing. She always wore a green ribbon around her neck.

There was a boy named Alfred in her class. Alfred liked Jenny, and Jenny liked Alfred.

One day he asked her, "Why do you wear that ribbon all the time?"

"I cannot tell you," said Jenny.

But Alfred kept asking.

"Why do you wear it?"

And Jenny would say, "It is not important."

Jenny and Alfred grew up and fell in love and got married. After their wedding, Alfred said, "Now that we are married, you must tell me about the green ribbon."

"You must still wait," said Jenny. "I will tell you when the right time comes."

Years passed. Alfred and Jenny grew old. One day Jenny became very sick. The doctor told her she was dying. Jenny called Alfred to her side.

"Alfred," she said, "now I can tell you about the green ribbon. Untie it, and you will see why I could not tell you before."

Slowly and carefully, Alfred untied the ribbon, and Jenny's head fell off.

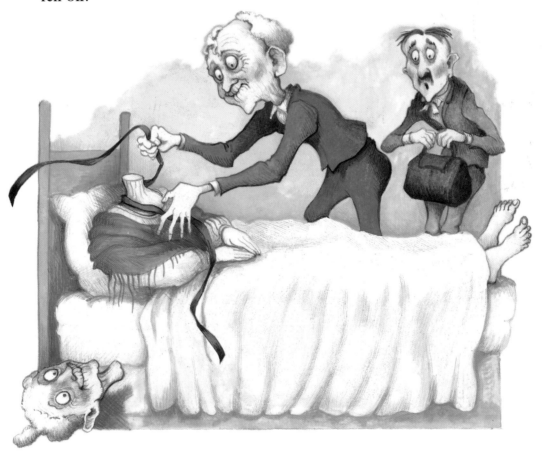

NOTES

LET'S GO! The haunted house or dwelling is a recurrent and popular setting for ghost stories. The "haunter" can be any creature from a genuine ghost to an imp to a poltergeist. A "boggart," as featured in this story that originates from northern England, and is variously attributed to Yorkshire or Lancashire, is a mischievous brownie, or one who, when provoked, turns from a help to a nuisance. For an exhaustive catalog of otherworldly beings, see Katharine Briggs's *Encyclopedia of Faeries: Hobgoblins, Brownies, Bogies, and Other Supernatural Creatures* (1978), where this story is recorded.

SPOOKS A-HUNTING Many ghost stories revolve around the consequences of a human's defying a ghost's wish or command. In this story, the human is chastened by the experience, whereas in other stories the human gets the better of the ghost, proving that ghosts are no smarter than the living persons they once were.

MY BIG TOE This story, featuring the spirit who comes back to claim a part of his body that was inadvertently exhumed, is a variant of a popular tale known in many parts of America. Sometimes called "The Hairy Toe," it is closely related to the well-known "Teeny-Tiny," as collected in Joseph Jacobs's *English Fairy Tales*, and also to the American "Taily-Po" (from West Virginia or Tennessee), in which the body part in question is the spirit's tail. Stories like these, with repeating lines that should be read louder and louder, are called "gotcha" stories, or "jump" stories, so-called because they make the listener jump.

'TAIN'T SO This story about the dead who won't stay that way originally appeared in Dr. John Bennett's *The Doctor to the Dead* (1943), a famous collection of tales about both white and black people from South Carolina. It is reprinted in the latter of Maria Leach's two fine collections of scary stories, *The Thing at the Foot of the Bed* and *Whistle in the Graveyard*, both excellent sources for more such tales.

THE MAN WHO WAS AFRAID OF NOTHING This Native American story originated with the Brulé Sioux tribe, a branch of the western Sioux nation that lived in the area that is now South Dakota. The story is remarkably similar to the Grimms' "A Tale of a Boy Who Set Out to Learn Fear" (Grimm 4), which shows how story themes reappear in cultures all around the world.

THE MERMAID The appearance of a mermaid is a rarity in African-American stories and demonstrates that these folktales, as told in America (this story was recorded in Michigan by the famous folklorist Richard M. Dorson), were influenced by other cultures, in this case European cultures, where mermaid stories are common. The dialect has been altered slightly for easier reading.

DAUNTLESS LITTLE JOHN This is an Italian version of a story that uses the common motif of the person brave enough to spend a night in a haunted place. Probably best known as the Spanish *Tinker and the Ghost*, the story has other variants. It features another motif that recurs in literature of the supernatural, namely the restless ghost, or revenant, who cannot rest until he expiates his sins, redresses a wrong, points the way to some treasure, or imparts information.

THE CONJURE WIVES It was the belief of some Africans who were brought to the United States and the West Indies that certain individuals, called variously conjure wives, conjure men or women, or conjure doctors, had supernatural powers and could work magic (or voodoo) with the aid of roots, herbs, and other ingredients. Francis Wickes's adaptation of this conjure tale appeared in *Holiday Stories*, 1921.

MR. MIACCA This tale of the evil boy-stealer is of English origin and was collected in Joseph Jacobs's *English Fairy Tales* (1889). It undoubtedly served as a cautionary tale. A whole subgenre of frightening tales, popularized as Gothics, revolves around the dreaded body snatchers, who not only stole corpses and jewels from graves but also murdered victims in order to supply newly dead bodies to medical schools or for some other nefarious purpose.

THE GOBLINS AT THE BATHHOUSE It was a commonly held belief that spirit figures of all kinds rose from their graves or their haunts only during the hours of darkness. The appearance of dawn signaled the loss of their visibility, and of their power.

THE GREEN RIBBON This simple story, an enduring favorite of children, may have its source, according to folklorist Alvin Schwartz, in a folk belief of the Middle Ages that a red thread worn around the neck marked the place where someone's head had fallen off and was then reattached.